Grolier Books is a division of Grolier Enterprises, Inc.

ISBN: 0-679-88157-3 (trade ed.) ; 0-679-98157-8 (lib. bdg.)
Library of Congress Catalog Card Number: 97-0066894

Printed in the United States of America   10 9 8 7 6 5 4 3 2 1

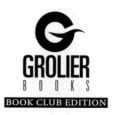

GROLIER
B O O K S
BOOK CLUB EDITION

Can You Tell Me How to Get to SESAME STREET?

by Eleanor Hudson

illustrated by
Joe Mathieu

BEGINNER BOOKS

A Division of Random House, Inc.

Elmo likes books.

Fat books.

Funny books.

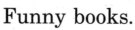

Bat books.

Bunny books.

Bear-in-the-chair books.

Kite-in-the-air books.

"Elmo will go fly a kite."

Where?

There!

High up in the air!

SWOOSH!

The wind takes the kite.

WHOOSH!

The kite takes Elmo.

Hold on tight!

Elmo the kite-flyer
flies higher
and higher.

Sesame Street gets smaller...

...and smaller.

Elmo looks up.

What does he see?

The birds in the clouds.

The clouds in the sky.

The sky all around.

But Elmo does not see Sesame Street.

Elmo looks down.

What does he see?

The ducks in the pond.

The pond in the park.

The park in the town

way, way down.

But Elmo does not see Sesame Street.

OOPS!

DOWN, DOWN, DOWN

he swoops!

Elmo lands smack
in the back
of a truck
full of ducks.

"Can you tell Elmo how to get
to Sesame Street?"

"*Quack, quack, quack!*"
is all the ducks say.

They don't know the way!

The truck hits a bump.
KER-THUMP!

Elmo falls—plop—
on top
of a log
lined with frogs.

"Can you tell Elmo how to get
to Sesame Street?"

"Ribbit, ribbit,"
the frogs go.

They don't know!

CRASH!

A wave takes Elmo.

SPLASH!

Elmo takes his kite.

Hang on tight!

Elmo lands splat on a mat—
just like that!

It waggles.
It glides.

It takes off.

He rides!

WHOOPS!
UP, UP, UP
he swoops!

Up to the stars.
Up to Mars!
Up to a place
in outer space.

Past the moon,
DOWN
DOWN
DOWN
Elmo zooms.

Earth gets BIGGER...

and BIGGER...

and BIGGER.

Elmo lands—
KER-PLUNK—
in a hunk
of green vines and gunk.

Hello.

It's a trunk!

"Can you tell Elmo how to get
to Sesame Street?"

Hip, hip, hooray!
The elephant shows
Elmo the way.

Where?

Past that bear in a lair.

Right out the gate,

not a moment too late.

Back to Sesame Street!

Elmo likes books.

Fairy tales.

Scary tales.

Sunny books.

Funny books.

Easy read-aloud books.

Elmo feels so proud.

Books!